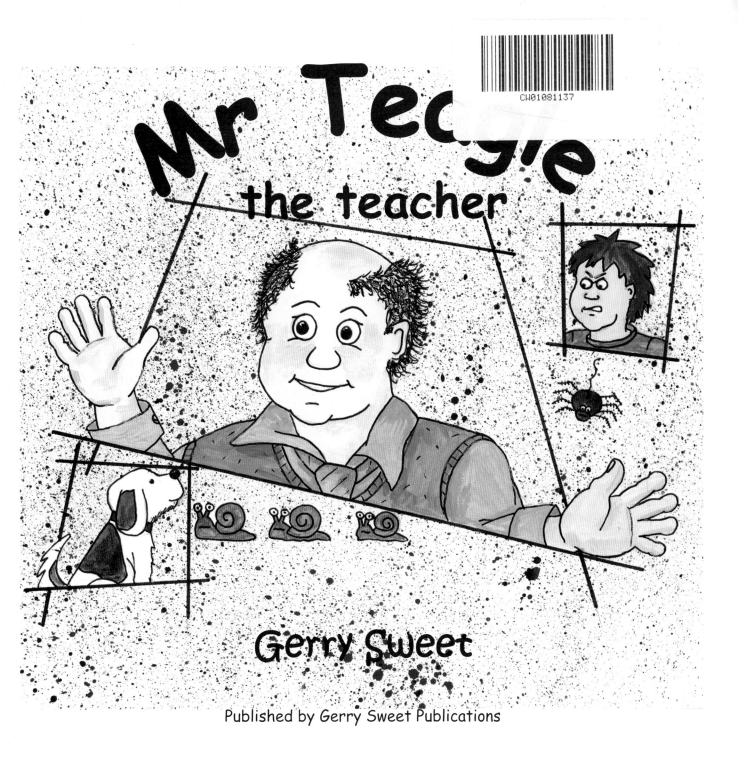

Mr Teague

the teacher

Gerry Sweet

Published by Gerry Sweet Publications

First published in Great Britain in 2007 by
Gerry Sweet Publications

Coom's Lodge,
Bolenna
Perrancoombe
Perranporth
Cornwall
TR6 OHT

ISBN 978-0-9555591-0-5

Acknowledgements:
Many thanks to
Stuart Odgers
Mat Williams
Special thanks to Paul Baker

Printed and bound in Great Britain by
Troutbeck Press, Mabe, Cornwall

Mr Teagle and
the naughty boy

When you were once a child going off to Primary School
playing with your friends and hoping you were cool,
thinking about computers and all the latest games
and asking mum and dad to buy the latest names.

As you sat at your desk and waited for your lunch
or made a plan for playtime about who would have a punch,
when none of your pens worked and your rubber had just been nicked
and the boy on the next table complained of being kicked.

Did you ever wonder how your teacher must be feeling
standing in the classroom, with his head touching the ceiling?
Wearing daft old socks and the world's untrendiest shoes
and with a tasteless jumper even your granny wouldn't choose.

Did you ever sit down when you had nothing to do
and wonder what life was like from a teacher's point of view?
With thirty pairs of eyes watching every move you make
and most of them just watching for that very first mistake.

Well here's a chance to show you what it's really all about,
why teachers sometimes laugh, often cry and usually shout.
This is the story of a teacher, Mr Teagle he is called,
he's 48, a little plump and very nearly bald.

He has always been a teacher since the age of 21
and every single year he has had loads of fun.
But all this was to change I'm so very sad to say
when a naughty new year 6 walked into his class one day.

Max, the naughty new boy, had been expelled three times,
once for fighting, once for spitting and making up rude rhymes.
Now he's arrived at Mr Teagle's school and never does his work,
he spends his time making sure the teachers go beserk.

Having a name like Teagle and very little hair
does save money on haircuts but is really quite unfair
when Max, the naughty year 6, shouts across the room to Teagle
"You look just like a light bulb and a very fat bald eagle!"

Before Max came to St Meriadoc School, Teagle always smiled
but the naughty Max has stopped all that and turned him really wild.
The children in his class used to be so good and quiet
but young Max Jones has messed things up and now it is a riot.

He always whistles in the class when it's a spelling test
and writes on his book front covers "Max Jones is the best".
When it is PE time he steals everybody's kit
and always puts drawing pins where the girls are about to sit.

He always goes to the toilet, of course without permission
because it's in the toilets where he has a secret mission.
He waits for a tiny infant to open up the door,
then sticks out his right leg so they crash down on the floor.

He never learns his tables or reads one reading book
and if you ever asked him to, you'd get a funny look.
He never takes his letters home which drives Teagle insane
and turns every homework sheet into a paper aeroplane.

If he spies your school ruler, he's bound to snap it in half
and if you dare to challenge him, you'll get a little laugh.
He's the bully of the playground who always likes to tease
'cos one of his favourite hobbies is tripping up year threes.

One day poor Mr Teagle was teaching class 6 art
when from the corner of the room was heard a massive fart.
It came from Max of course but he blamed it on James Whetter,
poor James was sent straight to the Head and sent home with a letter.

Mr Teagle's favourite lesson was teaching ICT
because when it came to computers the school had 23.
The children could log on and off and use Excel and Word
but trying to teach ICT to Max was really quite absurd.

If you were working next to him he'd call you a " little jerk"
and if you dared tell Teagle then he'd delete all of your work.
He'd spit all over your keyboard and scratch all of the screen,
he really was the naughtiest boy the school had ever seen.

One morning in assembly he opened the classroom door,
took the dinner register and hid it in his drawer.
So when it came to lunchtime no one could have a lunch
and if you dared tell Teagle then you'd get a Max Jones punch.

If Max had a favourite lesson then Golden Time was it,
he'd spend his morning working out were he was going to sit.
He'd move up to the toys that he knew cost loads of money,
smash them on the ground and shout out "That was really funny!!"

Then there was the "accident" with Teagle's cup of tea
that he left in the classroom when he was teaching ICT.
Max went into the classroom and poured in some pen ink
and waited for his teacher to return and have a drink.

When the poor man had a sip he gave a funny look,
sat down on his teacher's chair and shut his reading book.
He rushed off to the toilets with his face all sweaty and red
and spent the next two weeks lying in a hospital bed.

This really was the last straw, Colin Teagle had had enough,
this new year six called Max Jones had made his life so rough.
He put down all his marking which he'd brought home in five sacks
and started to think hard how he could get revenge on Max.

He didn't sleep a wink that night, planning what to do,
thinking about the cup of tea and how Max broke the loo,
remembering all the drawing pins and broken Golden Time toys
and how Max really was the very naughtiest of boys.

In the morning he was happy with the idea that he had,
maybe not a masterpiece but, then again, not bad.
He would create class monitors starting from tomorrow,
could this be a way to turn Max's joy to sorrow?

Charlotte could collect the books and Jamie give them out,
if the infants had a fight then Alanah could sort it out.
Cameron could tidy maths books and Tegen sharpen pencils
and Sam could be in charge of looking for lost stencils.

But Max was given a job that really was quite cruel,
designed to upset him so much he'd go and leave the school.
Whenever it was raining really really hard
he had to go and collect up all the rubbish from the yard.

Well this was working brilliantly, everything going to plan,
Mr Teagle was just thinking he was such a clever man.
Max would come in soaking, sit in the class and splutter
and he felt too wet and miserable to even make a mutter.

All the class was happy and Teagle was relieved,
thinking of all the good things his idea had achieved.
But just when Max Jones was almost ready now to leave
something strange happened that no one could believe.

On a wet and wild playtime when all the class were in
and Max was collecting rubbish and putting it in the bin,
Max looked down on the ground... and something looked quite funny,
that wasn't rubbish he'd picked up, just loads and loads of money.

A fiver here, a tenner there and then a twenty pound note,
he found so much he picked it up and stuffed them in his coat.
He ran back to class and opened the door without a sound
then Max announced he'd found three hundred pounds out on the ground.

The children were so sad that night when they all went away,
the worst news of all, it meant that Max was here to stay.
Teagle was annoyed that his first plan was in tatters
"I've got to get rid of that boy, that's all that really matters!"

Plan number two was a cracker and involved the whole school play,
surely this would drive that horrible Max Jones right away!
The play was Peter Pan and before they all could start
Mr Teagle had to ensure that they all were given a part.

Everyone was thrilled when they all were given their parts
and they all wanted to know the actual date when it all starts.
All that is except Max who could only sob and yell
when Teagle announced that he would play the part of Tinkerbell.

Teagle knew that Max in a dress and fairy wings
would really be to him one of the most embarrassing things.
The hope was he would fly around with a fairy wand in his hand
and the children would all make a laugh that he simply couldn't stand.

He no longer would be known as the tough guy of the school,
the boys who ducks all children in the local swimming pool.
The bully who NEVER loses any of his fights
cos no one would be scared of a fairy wearing tights.

The play finally started and Teagle sat and waited
to finally see the downfall of the only boy he'd hated.
But after the second scene Teagle's happiness turned to rage
when everybody cheered when the fairy came on stage.

Just when Teagle thought that his plan was working well,
a standing ovation was given to that fairy Tinkerbell.
"He's the star of the show, it's a part he's really nailed".
The teacher then realised that another plan had failed.

Teagle was resigned to accepting a huge defeat,
he really couldn't get rid of this bully and this cheat.
He knew that Max had won and he couldn't work out why,
they were stuck with each other now 'til the end of July.

Max's pranks and teasing got worse and worse each day,
he got hold of the Smartboard and even painted it grey.
He found Teagle's car keys and hid them under the door
so his teacher had to sleep that night on his classroom floor.

When all the other children were going out to play,
in the nature garden Max would be digging away.
He'd find loads of snails that were all very juicy and runny
and chuck them at the girls and think that it was funny.

If you played him at chess and if he happened to lose
He'd dig up a hairy spider and hide it in your shoes.
If he really didn't like you, you'd get a great big punch
and he'd wipe all his snot on your sandwiches at lunch.

If you wonder why the Head didn't expel naughty Max
she had to, didn't she, when she knew all of the facts?
It really was a secret but…if you must know all the truth…
Mrs Waterhouse, the Head teacher, was Max's Aunty Ruth.

Although she knew Max could be very naughty at times,
she turned a blind eye to nearly all his crimes.
She would do all she could to stick up for that naughty lad
and would never admit that he'd been so very bad.

One day Marlo the Magician turned up for the whole day
as a treat for all the children who'd done so well in the play.
He asked for a volunteer to help him on the stage
and chose naughty Max which filled everyone with rage.

Mr Teagle was angry, upset and very sad
"Why has he chosen the boy who is so bad?
He could have chosen anyone else in our school
but he's gone and picked the school's complete and utter fool!"

But Marlo the Magician gave Teagle a quick wink,
waved his wand twice and then Max Jones turned pink.
He uttered the magic word "Wickettywickettywoke"
and then Max disappeared in a great big puff of smoke.

Now that was the end of Max Jones from year Six
and it was truly the greatest of Marlo's wonderful tricks.
He was never seen again but no one ever did mind
now Teagle's the Head cos Mrs Waterhouse resigned.

But what happened next I really do not know
after that great trick...where did Max Jones go?
Surely a magician isn't really quite that clever
that he can make a naughty year six disappear forever?

So when you're back in class in the next week or two
and a strange new boy arrives and sits down next to you.
Have a close look at him and remember this short tale
and check all of his pockets for a nice big juicy snail!!!

Mr Teagle and
the new puppy

Teachers love teaching their classes all day,
they do it for fun, not just for the pay.
Teaching children to learn is really fantastic
unless you end up with Max, then it is drastic.

Now a secret I'll tell you but don't breathe a word,
I'll tell you a fact that I once overheard.
When the end of term comes and the children depart,
teachers' favourite time is when the holidays start.

They all wave goodbye to their pupils at last,
tidy the room up and leave really fast.
They drive to their houses, collapse on their beds
and take lots of tablets for their aching heads.

Then they wake up, all fresh and renewed,
get dressed, come downstairs and eat lots of food.
As they wash all the dishes and wipe all the pans
they think about all of their holiday plans.

Mr Teagle, a teacher at St Meriadoc School
loved all his holidays and thought they were cool.
He usually spent 5 and a half weeks in France
but this summer he wouldn't be given the chance.

This year his holiday just wouldn't be the same,
he'd bought a new puppy and given it a name.
Jabber he called it cos it barked all the time,
you'd think that a burglar was committing a crime.

This puppy was tiny, 'bout the size of a rabbit
but really it had a most terrible habit.
Whenever it was taken for a walk round the street
it thought it could take on any dog it would meet.

It could be an Alsatian, Boxer, Great Dane,
Jabber would run at the speed of a train
up to these giants and prepare for a fight,
then see their huge size and run off with a fright.

One morning they decided to go for a walk
off into town to buy Teagle some chalk.
Just as they walked past the old butcher's shop
Jabber spied an old woman with a tasty lamb chop.

Quick as a flash he broke from his lead,
he couldn't miss out on this chance for a feed.
He sprinted behind her without making a sound
and pushed the poor woman so she fell to the ground.

Now Jabber was tiny without any fat
but he'd finished the chop in 30 seconds flat.
He spotted another and downed that as well
just as the poor woman gave a terrified yell.

Her walking stick went flying up into the air
and her glasses fell off, there was glass everywhere.
Her false teeth ended up in Mrs Pascoe's garden
forcing Teagle to shout " Oh I do beg your pardon!"

This woman called Gladys was not badly hurt,
she got up from the ground and shook off the dirt.
She picked up her handbag and checked all her money
and did something then that you might think quite funny.

She picked up her walking stick which lay on the ground
and swung her right arm around and around.
She hit Mr Teagle on the leg and the chest
and called a policeman who made an arrest.

Teagle was handcuffed and taken away
and put in a police cell where he did have to stay
for an hour and a half in the company of cops
while Gladys told them all about her vanishing chops.

The poor teacher was then fined 68 pounds,
which doesn't sound much but is more than it sounds
when you are a teacher earning 2 pounds an hour
a large fine like that leaves you feeling quite sour.

When he'd recovered from the shock of it all
and Jabber had punctured another football.
He turned on the tv for "Ready Steady Cook"
and decided he ought to mark a maths book.

He picked up a red pen and found the right page
and then flew into an uncontrollable rage.
The maths books he kept by the comfy settee
were all soaking wet and covered in wee.

Jabber the puppy had been up to his tricks
and this was a problem even Marlo couldn't fix.
The children next term would all go beserk
when told that a dog's weed on all of their work.

This was not the holiday Teagle hoped it would be,
first there was Gladys and now loads of wee.
Things could only get better but oh no, alas,
he looked out of his window to find holes in the grass.

Teagle was sad cos his garden was great
and then he met his neighbour in a terrible state.
He peered over the fence, slowly opening his eyes
and found to his astonishment and horrible surprise...

Jabber wasn't just happy with one hole or two,
in next door's garden he'd dug 32!
Mrs Bishop the neighbour was so proud of her lawn,
now Teagle the teacher wished he'd never been born.

She picked up her spade and made a quick run,
really annoyed at what Jabber had done.
"I'm sure Jabber didn't really mean any harm,"
he shouted as he got a spade in the arm.

He ran for his front door as fast as he could,
trying to avoid any more flying wood.
As he locked his front door, shaking just like a jelly
he tripped over Jabber who was watching the telly.

His glass of red wine spilled all over the floor
and he couldn't move for an hour cos his ankle was sore.
As he struggled to get up from under the settee
he realised he was lying in Jabber's wet wee.

Buying Jabber the puppy seemed so right at the time
but here he was blamed for every crime.
He'd been longing so much for his holiday to start
now he wished he was back in his school teaching art.

One day Mr Rogers came to Teagle's house to chat,
he was the new Headteacher of the school he was at.
Teagle gave him a drink and they sat down for chats
about teacher stuff like detention and Sats.

Jabber wouldn't settle, he stared at this Head,
then quick as a flash he jumped up from his bed.
Something must be wrong, why was Jabber staring?
Then he tugged with all his might at the wig he was wearing.

Mr Rogers' hair which his wife did adore
was now lying around on the living room floor.
Mr Rogers looked ashamed, like a naughty schoolboy
but Jabber didn't mind... he'd got a new toy.

Then there really started a most terrible commotion
and Rogers stopped talking 'bout Teagle's promotion.
He picked up his wig and stuffed it in his pocket,
slammed the front door shut and drove off like a rocket.

Teagle went to bed that night depressed and sad,
surely life's not meant to be always so bad?
His dreams were full of nightmares about naughty dog bites,
this really had been the most horrible of nights.

He was woken by more barking it gave him a fright,
this Jabber never stopped in the daytime or night.
But Jabber wouldn't stop, Teagle couldn't sleep a wink
so he had to go downstairs to have a little drink.

Suddenly he heard noises coming from next door,
surely Mrs Bishop was on holiday in Singapore?
Jabber wouldn't settle and wanted to go out
when from next door there came a bump and a shout.

Jabber ran in the garden and straight over the fence,
Teagle followed on tiptoe feeling very tense.
A burglar in a dark suit was carrying stuff away,
the teacher shouted "Come back boy" but he didn't obey.

The burglar started running when he saw the dog near,
he may be just a small dog but he filled him with fear.
Then suddenly the burglar did two forward rolls,
he had tripped over one of Jabber's new holes.

The burglar couldn't move and soon gave himself up
and blamed all his bad luck on "That pesky little pup!!"
The police, who now knew Teagle, arrived for the arrest
and Teagle went indoors in order to get dressed.

The newspapers the next day all mentioned this story,
Teagle was photographed in all of his glory.
The noisy dog and teacher, still in his dressing gown
were now the local heroes and the talk of the town.

An interview on GMTV was given to them that day,
Teagle saying how they scared the burglar away.
Jabber was given a bone which he then went and hid
and Teagle was rewarded with nine hundred quid.

"What an incredible holiday!" thought Teagle that night
as he went up to bed, turning off the light.
"So many things have happened, some serious, some funny
but who'd have thought I'd end up with all of that money".

As he dreamed a lovely dream about becoming so rich,
Jabber was in the garden digging another ditch.
Not for a juicy bone to eat for tomorrow's tea
but to hide the 900 pounds he'd chewed and soaked in wee.

Mr Teagle and
the birthday party

The holidays ended after 6 super weeks,
back to school went the teacher with large chubby cheeks
to see all the teachers and meet his new class,
relieved there were no more holes in his grass.

No more police fines and no more arrests,
no more inky drinks and no year 6 pests.
This year was going to be free from disaster,
Mr Rogers was sacked leaving him as headmaster.

His pay had gone up again and again,
he really was one of the luckiest of men
to be in charge of a school that gave him great fun,
if life was a pop chart then he'd be number one.

But this morning he wasn't even thinking 'bout school,
not Sats nor behaviour or any new rule.
As he parked his new car just inside the gate,
he thought about Saturday, he just couldn't wait.

This Saturday you see was a very special day,
he was looking forward to the "hip hip hooray"
from all of his friends as they stood in a line
and threw him a party as he reached 49.

The big day arrived and Teagle was glad,
he spent all the morning with his old mum and dad
who had given him some money but luckily no top,
cos after last year's jumper Teagle told them to stop.

All afternoon he had spent baking his cake
which made him so nervous he started to shake,
so he needed some help from Great Auntie Gertie
before everyone arrived at about 7.30.

Everyone arrived on time at his house,
Jabber was being good, as quiet as a mouse.
Gladys arrived with her present..........a cup
and a tasty lamb chop for Jabber the pup.

Mrs Bishop arrived and was full of big smiles,
she'd come from Singapore which is hundreds of miles.
She'd bought Teagle sweets and a tub of popcorn
and a book about how to look after your lawn.

Marlo turned up with a book full of tricks,
"How to make children disappear" was found on page six.
The teachers arrived as it just started raining
with a book that was called " Basic dog training".

Then Teagle went to carry in his birthday cake
that Great Auntie Gertie had helped him to bake.
But he tripped on a book which lay on the floor
and half of the cake ended up out the door.

Now there was half a cake for everyone to eat
but at least it gave Jabber a nice tasty treat
cos he ate all the slices that were now on the floor,
then barked at his master when he wanted some more.

The candles were lit and placed on the cake
by old Mrs Teagle whose hands rather shake
so she missed all the candles and set fire to her dress
then ran up the stairs to quickly undress.

Soon there was panic, a fire started to roar,
everyone sprinted to get to the door.
A fire engine arrived and put out the flame
and poor Mrs Teagle escaped any blame.

The house soon was sorted and all tidied up
except for balloons that were burst by the pup.
The party could re start at 8.25
and everyone was glad that they were still alive.

"Pass the parcel" was Teagle's game number 1,
a game that he knew would give everyone fun.
But as the game ended, everyone sighed,
he'd forgotten to leave a present inside.

They played some more games and ate loads of food,
there were only 2 presents that young Jabber chewed.
A car engine was heard roaring onto the drive,
Teagle wondered when the DJ was going to arrive.

With Bermuda shorts, a t shirt and hat,
the DJ walked in and started to chat
to all of the guests before he played the 1st song,
then Teagle noticed that something was wrong.

The DJ he'd found in the telephone book
was really quite scary... but it wasn't his look
which brought back a memory which to Teagle was bad,
the DJ he'd hired was Max Jones' dad.

Steve Jones was a DJ you could hire for a gig,
he looked just like Max but three times as big.
But he'd never met Teagle before in his life
or knew that this teacher had given Max strife.

Teagle had a panic and started to shake
and thought every bone in his body would break.
When DJ Steve Jones finds out he'd be bitter
when he hears he forced Max to pick up the litter.

Teagle downed red wine, one glass and then two,
after 5 glasses he had to sprint to the loo.
He was running too fast that he slipped on some mud
and fell to the floor with a crash and a thud.

The last thing he remembered he had just left the loo
but what happened next...he hadn't a clue.
On his 49th birthday this poor old headmaster
woke up in hospital with his leg in a plaster.

He couldn't believe his bad luck again,
the day started with laughter and ended with pain.
The party was great he was having a laugh,
he enjoyed spending time with his friends and the staff.

He remembered his panic when he saw Max's dad
and expected that he would go totally mad.
But really Steve Jones was in the police
and was a great believer in keeping the peace.

He needn't have panicked and ended up in bed,
Steve Jones wouldn't have hurt a hair on his head.
Six years before he started his criminal search,
DJ Steve used to work as the vicar of a church.

Teagle lay on his bed and thought for a while
about Peter Pan which did make him smile,
when a nurse came in and asked with a grin
if an old friend of his could actually come in.

"Of course" said the teacher, "it'll cheer me up,
I haven't seen anyone...not even my pup".
Then Teagle looked up with shock and surprise
at the visitor who stood smiling in front of his eyes.

"Hello Mr Teagle, I heard you weren't well, "
said young Max Jones, who had made his life hell.
"I'm sorry I was naughty...I won't do it again,
I've brought you some chocolates to take away the pain".

"When Marlo gave the spell I ran out the door
but I promise you that I'm not naughty any more.
I'm now going to that school just down the street
and I'm polite and well mannered to everyone I meet".

"You were a great teacher and I really was bad,
I know I was the worst boy that you've ever had.
So I bought you some chocs to put it all right,
now it's late and I've got so much homework tonight."

And with that he left and Teagle was happy,
young Max really was quite a nice chappy.
That visit was one of his biggest ever shocks
cos Max is now good and he bought him some chocs.

He sat up in bed and opened the box,
his best present of all was truly these chocs.
He opened the lid.. THAT MAX JONES WAS A THUG!
THERE WEREN'T ANY CHOCS.....JUST 5 SNAILS AND A SLUG!!!

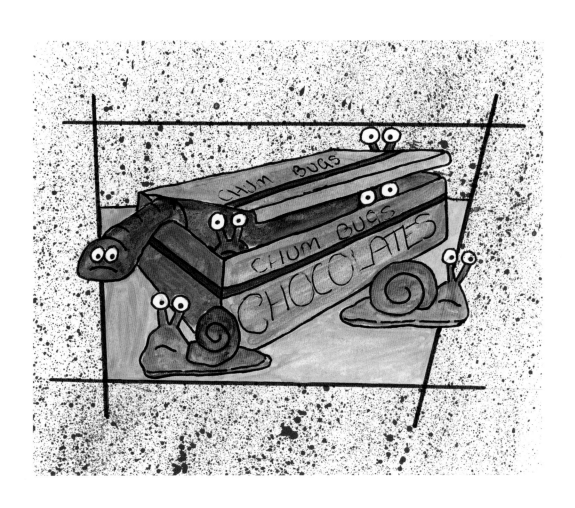

For Charlotte and Jamie with love

About the Author

Gerry Sweet, like Mr Teagle, is a teacher in Cornwall. He is married to Ruth and has two children, Charlotte and Jamie. Just like Mr Teagle, he loves his job, likes walking his dog and really looks forward to his summer holidays.